Polly P~~~~~n

GIN~~ ~~~~~ON

Illustrated by
JACQUI THOMAS

HEINEMANN · LONDON

For the Double Class Room at
SS Philip and James First School, Oxford

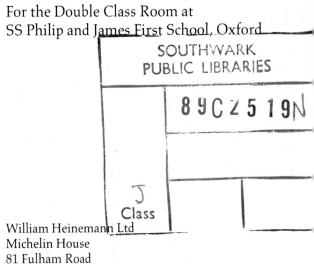

William Heinemann Ltd
Michelin House
81 Fulham Road
London SW3 6RB

LONDON   MELBOURNE   AUCKLAND

First published 1989
Text © 1989 Gina Wilson
Illustrations © 1989 Jacqui Thomas

ISBN 0 434 93050 4
Produced by Mandarin Offset
Printed and bound in Hong Kong

A school pack of BANANAS 31-36
is available from
Heinemann Educational Books
ISBN 0 435 001051

Chapter One

POLLY PEAKE'S BROTHER and sister were older than she was and they seemed to be cleverer at absolutely everything. Mrs Peake comforted Polly by saying that they had had longer to learn, and that one day she would catch them up. But Polly couldn't wait. She was short and plump and iron-willed, and she wanted to be the cleverest at something *now*.

Secretly, she had the feeling that she might be rather good at music. Mrs King, the music teacher at school, had always praised her singing and recently something really exciting had happened. After school one day she had picked up a recorder, left behind by someone else, and given it a little blow.

She had expected it to squeak or screech.
But it hadn't! A pure sound had poured
out of it at once! She had tried again –
but now it *had* turned squeaky. Again –
and now it *did* screech. But she kept
remembering that first, wonderful
stream of sound. If she had done it once,
she could do it again.

It was almost Polly's ninth birthday.
'I think I'd like a recorder for my
present,' she said one breakfast time.
'Yes. That's what I really want, please.'

'But nobody in the family plays the

recorder,' said Louise, crunching cornflakes. 'If you take up gymnastics I can help you.'

Tom licked marmalade off his fingers. 'I could teach you chess.'

But Mr and Mrs Peake bought Polly a recorder, and Mrs King allowed her to come along to the recorder group, just to watch. 'It's easy,' she said, 'like sums and writing and anything, really, as long as you keep trying.'

'Oh!' Polly looked doubtful. Nothing was easy about sums and writing. And 'trying' was downright difficult. People often thought she wasn't trying, even when she knew she was. 'It's no good if you won't try,' Mrs Peake had sighed, unravelling woolly knots in Polly's knitting. And 'You're not *trying*,' Louise and Tom had exploded over the Scrabble board. 'Anyone above the age of two can spell *bicycle*!'

Polly watched Mrs King conducting the recorder group. Mrs King swayed and hummed and counted one-two-three. She tapped her feet and flapped her hands and, at the end, she sat down with a bump and ran her fingers through her thick, curly hair. 'What did you think of that, Polly?'

'Great!' breathed Polly. 'Can I join next week?'

'We'll see,' said Mrs King. 'You'll have to try very hard.'

But this didn't worry Polly any more. Skinny Vincent Darrah was in the recorder group and everyone knew he never tried very hard. Nor did tiny Fred Botkol, or Emma Thornton, who kept playing one-handed because she needed the other to push her glasses up her nose. Polly knew that if they could do it,

so could she.

At the end of the afternoon, she stood by the main school door waiting for her mum. She was trying different fingers over the holes of her recorder. 'You're getting the hang of that, all right!' said Mr Mulligan, the caretaker. 'You're what they call a natural.' He and Polly were friends. Mrs Peake was often late collecting Polly because her job didn't finish until three o'clock. Polly talked to Mr Mulligan then. Sometimes, he let her polish the cloakroom floor by skidding about on it with dusters tied

round her feet. He said she was "a natural" at that, too. Mr Mulligan had a limp in one leg and didn't really like bending down.

That afternoon, Mrs Peake was flustered as usual. 'For pity's sake, stop tooting that thing down my ear!' she said in the car. 'I'm tired.'

'Mrs King says I've got to keep trying.'

'Well, try later.'

Mrs Peake stopped frowning when she'd had her cup of tea. She had bought a special book which told you how to play different notes on the recorder. There were pictures of someone's fingers covering the holes so you could check you were doing the same. By the time Louise and Tom came in from school, Polly could play several notes and knew what their names were.

'Show off!' said Tom.

'That's not a tune!' said Louise, but they both smiled at Polly anyway, to show they were only teasing.

'They don't want you to get big-headed,' whispered Mrs Peake. 'They can see you're good at this.'

After that, Polly became better and better and soon Mrs King let her stand beside Vincent Darrah in the recorder group and play with the others.

'Smarty pants!' hissed Vincent. 'Think you're good, don't you?' He

swayed from side to side and knocked
Polly's recorder against her teeth so it
squeaked.

'I'll get you for that,' said Polly. She
had learnt a thing or two from Louise
and Tom. She kicked him on the ankle
and he roared aloud.

'Vincent, step out!' Mrs King roared
back, still conducting the others. 'This is
a lullaby.'

'She kicked me, Miss. Polly Peake
kicked me right on the ankle bone.'

But Polly was playing like an angel

now she had room for her elbows. Mrs King let her stay. 'You're learning very quickly,' she said as they packed up at the end. 'Does your family like listening to you?'

'I think so,' said Polly. 'None of them can play the recorder.'

'Nor can you,' scoffed Vincent after Mrs King had gone. 'Your fingers are like sausages.'

'No, they aren't,' said Emma Thornton stoutly. 'Polly's the best recorder player in the school!'

Chapter Two

VINCENT DARRAH WAS in very
low spirits. He had been looking
forward to being the star of the end-of-
term Christmas concert. Some time ago,
Mrs King had promised him a solo. She
had said she would like him to play the
first verse of "Little Donkey" all by
himself in front of the parents. 'You'll
surprise everybody, Vincent,' she had
said, gazing at him warmly. 'They don't
know half the good things you can do.
But *I* know.' That was *before* Polly
Peake had turned into a genius . . .

Polly knew nothing of this. Secretly,
she was dying for Mrs King to ask *her* to
play a solo. Just imagine! The whole
family would sit there, clapping like
mad! She practised and practised. 'Mind
you don't overdo it on that thing,' said

Tom, popping his head round the door.
'You'll blow your brains out – if you've
got any.'

'He's impressed really!' said Louise.
'So am I.'

'It'll be lovely to see you in the
Christmas concert,' whispered Mrs
Peake. 'Gran's staying with us that
night. She'll enjoy it, too.'

'Yippee!' shouted Polly.

After school, every day, she played
her recorder to Mr Mulligan. 'You're a
champ on that,' he said. 'You'll be

playing a solo at the concert. I'll bring Mrs Mulligan, just to hear you.'

'But Mrs King hasn't asked me yet,' said Polly.

'She will.'

And she did. 'Vincent is playing a solo at the beginning,' she said to Polly. 'And I'd like you to finish the concert off with another one.'

'Can I play "Hark the Herald"?' said Polly. 'That's my favourite.'

Mrs Peake was delighted. 'I *knew* Mrs King would ask you, Polly. I'll phone Gran to make sure she can come. When she came off the phone, she was pink with excitement. 'Gran's sending

you a special recorder,' she said. 'It's an old one that Great Uncle George used to play. She says you can have it in plenty of time for the concert.'

'But Great Uncle George is dead,' said Polly. 'It'll make me think of ghosts. It'll be all old and battered.'

'It'll sound beautiful,' said Mrs Peake. 'That's the important thing.'

During the next few days, Polly tried not to think of Great Uncle George and his recorder, but people kept reminding her.

'Poor you!' whispered Tom. 'Great Uncle George had whiskers and bad teeth!'

Even Louise had her doubts. 'His recorder might be full of germs after all these years.'

'I'm going to get cross,' said Mrs Peake, getting cross. 'We can easily clean it up. Polly's very lucky. Old instruments sound best.'

Polly still felt worried. Secretly, she began to hope the recorder might get lost in the post.

But it didn't. One afternoon, Mrs Peake came rushing into school with it in its own tattered leather case. She and

Mr Mulligan sat on a bench beside the coat pegs and examined it. 'Mr Mulligan has promised to keep it in his locker for you when you bring it to school,' said Mrs Peake. 'You can't stuff it in your drawer with dirty hankies and pencil shavings and things.'

'My drawer's nice and tidy,' said Polly.

'Give us a tune,' said Mr Mulligan. 'Let's hear it.'

Polly shuddered. The recorder was wooden, a pale fawn colour. Round the end where she had to blow, there seemed to be teethmarks – Tom would say they were, anyway. She closed her eyes and started to play.

'Oh, my!' said Mr Mulligan.

'Oh, Polly!' gasped Mrs Peake. 'It's magic! It's like a fairy pipe!'

Polly thought so, too. Her heart was

thumping with excitement. 'I'm always going to play it with my eyes shut, so I can pretend it is.'

After that, Polly played Uncle George's recorder at all the rehearsals for the concert. She loved its soft, pure sound; it never squeaked. 'You look batty with your eyes shut,' said Vincent Darrah. 'I don't think it's made of wood at all. I think it's one of your Uncle

George's old dead bones. Sounds like it anyway.'

'Shut up,' said Amy Strong, who didn't like anybody that day because she thought nobody liked her. 'You both sound horrible. There shouldn't be any solos at all. It's not fair.'

The concert was to be held in the evening in a church hall some distance from the school. The church hall was bigger than the one at school, and would hold a bigger audience. That week, the weather, which had been mild, suddenly

turned arctic. Mr Mulligan's leg ached so much that he grumbled at everyone. He even complained about wet wellingtons, saying he wasn't paid extra to clean up the puddles they made. On the day of the concert, as she was leaving school, Polly whispered in his ear that she hoped he and Mrs Mulligan would enjoy it. 'I'm not sure we can come,' he muttered. 'I'm in that much pain.' So Polly went quietly away and put her coat on but, at the last minute, he came limping towards her, smiling. 'You'll show 'em how it's done, Poll. I know you will.'

Mrs Peake was early that day. She was sitting in the car at the school gate, chatting to Gran. 'This is your big day,' said Gran as Polly climbed in. 'How do you feel?'

'Fine,' said Polly. 'Even Vincent's

been nice today. He gave me a
thumbs-up sign at the last rehearsal,
and I gave him one, too.'

Chapter Three

IT WAS BANG in the middle of tea
that Polly suddenly realised . . . It was a
special tea, with ice-cream *and* chocolate
biscuits instead of "either/or". Louise
and Tom were tucking into it, too.
'You're going to be fantastic, Poll,'
Louise had said. 'We'll keep our fingers
crossed.' Gran had just said, 'How are
you getting on with Uncle George's
recorder?' and Polly had begun to

answer, 'Fine, I . . .' when it dawned on her – *the recorder was still in Mr Mulligan's locker.*

Clutching her middle, Polly jumped up from her chair and rushed out of the room. 'Nerves,' she heard Gran murmur kindly. 'Poor little lass.'

In the hall, Polly threw on her coat and, in a bound, she was out of the house. The roads were quiet; it wasn't

too far; if she ran like mad, she could be
there and back before they finished tea.
Nobody must ever know what a
scatterbrain she was. 'To Polly!' Tom
had said, toasting her in Coca Cola. It
had all been perfect.

Polly tore along the pavement. The
wind made her nose run. Her breath
puffed out behind her into the dark.
When she reached the school, the door
was locked and all the lights were out,
but they were on at Mr Mulligan's
house, nearby. Polly knocked and he
opened the door. 'Oh, Mr Mulligan, I've
got to get into the school,' she gasped.

'I've left my recorder in your locker.'

'Can't you borrow another one, dear?' said Mrs Mulligan over Mr Mulligan's shoulder.

'It's my Great Uncle George's. Gran gave it to me. She's come a hundred miles specially to hear me play it tonight . . .' Polly's lip quivered.

Very slowly, Mr Mulligan fetched his

coat. 'He's not well,' whispered Mrs
Mulligan, looking worried. 'I would
come with you instead, only he likes to
do all the locking up himself.'

Mr Mulligan hobbled along on his
stick. Polly didn't dare speak to him as
they battled through the wind. She was
scared she might tell him to hurry up,
by mistake. At last they arrived. He
fumbled with the frozen lock and shone
his torch round, looking for a light
switch. 'Thank you. *Thank you!*' said
Polly as he handed her the leather
recorder-case. Then she was off,

hugging it to her chest, racing back the way she had come.

She made it! There was no sign of Dad's bike. He still wasn't back from work! Polly shoved at the ricketty gate. 'Close it behind you,' Mum always said. 'Specially when it's windy. We don't want it blown off its hinges.' Polly turned to fix the latch. A gust of wind caught the gate suddenly and slammed it shut – right on the third finger of her left hand . . .

Soon after that, it *was* like a sausage –
a blue one. It swelled and swelled till it
was twice its normal size.

'Can fingers burst?' Tom whispered
to Louise.

Mrs Peake made Polly hold it under
the cold tap. 'That'll soon bring it
down,' she said. 'Can you wiggle it?'

'No,' wailed Polly.

'You'll have to play the recorder with
your other fingers, then,' said Gran.

'I can't! That's not how you do it.'

In the midst of the hubbub, Mr Peake

walked in. He looked at the finger and then he looked sadly at Polly. 'I'm afraid you won't be able to play at all,' he said.

The Peakes went to the concert, anyway, all six of them. 'I know it's disappointing,' whispered Mrs Peake, 'but perhaps Mrs King will let you sing in the choir, instead.'

'I haven't learnt the words,' mumbled Polly. 'This is the worst day of my life.' She had a lump in her throat as hard as a

cherry stone. She sat between
Louise and Tom and made
herself clap every item on the
programme. Vincent Darrah played
'Little Donkey' with only two mistakes.
His applause lasted one minute thirty-
five seconds on Tom's watch. Mrs King
made Vincent bow, and two ladies
behind Polly leaned their heads together
and said it was a miracle!

After that, a singing-group

performed a carol and Jacob Mullen accompanied them on the glockenspiel, when he remembered to stop grinning at his mum and dad and get on with it.

Then came the recorder group, the percussion band, and the reception class, in tartan kilts, doing a Highland Fling.

'How's your finger, Poll?' asked Mrs Peake. 'Is there any hope?'

Polly looked down at the throbbing, blue sausage and shook her head. 'I'm glad Mr Mulligan didn't come,' she said. 'He would have been disappointed too.'

There was lots of singing in the second half. Amy Strong stood in the front row and sang so loudly that people thought she had a solo when she hadn't.

'What a show-off!' said Tom and pulled a face till Mr Peake got cross and made him stop.

At the very end, Mrs King stood up

and told everyone how sad it was that
Polly Peake had hurt her finger and
couldn't play for them. 'You've missed a
treat,' she said. 'It's something to look
forward to another day.' Everyone
clapped, and the people who knew the
Peakes turned round and looked at Polly
who was suddenly turning bright pink
with pleasure.

Chapter Four

THE NEXT DAY, Polly was late for school. 'Tell Miss Pringle it took you twice as long to do your buttons up, now you're a finger short,' said Mrs Peake.

Polly ran in through the school gates and stopped. In the middle of the playground stood a white police car. Inside, a policeman was holding a

walkie-talkie to his mouth. More policemen were in the school hall. Polly hung her coat on her peg and scurried along to the classroom.

'The school's been burgled!' Amy Strong shouted as soon as Polly opened the door.

'Be quiet, Amy,' snapped Miss Pringle.

'They've taken the computer!' called Vincent Darrah.

'And the video recorder!' yelled Jacob Mullen.

'And the projector!' whispered Fred Botkol.

'That's enough!' exploded Miss Pringle. 'Not another word!'

'I wonder if they'll send us home,' said Emma Thornton, who couldn't have been listening. 'Maybe we'll get the day off.'

Policemen were busy in school all morning. They wrote things down in special notebooks and talked in low voices. Amy Strong claimed one of them was her uncle, but nobody believed her. The shortest one, who was fat and looked like anybody's dad, turned out to be the most important of them all. He asked lots of people the same question. 'Who do you think locks up the school each night?'

'Mr Mulligan,' said everyone. 'Of course.'

'Oh dear!' thought Polly deep inside. 'Oh dear! OH DEAR!'

And, after school that day, Mr Mulligan wasn't there.

He wasn't there the next day, either.

'He might never come back,' said Emma Thornton sadly. 'Mrs Mulligan told my mum he thinks people are saying he didn't lock up properly. He thinks they're blaming him for the burglary. That's why he's staying off.'

'I think I'll stay off too,' mumbled Fred Botkol. 'I like Mr. Mulligan.'

'Oh dear!' thought Polly. She was so worried, she couldn't eat her lunch. She couldn't play the recorder even though her finger wasn't swollen any more. She couldn't do her lessons.

Mrs Peake thought she looked pale. 'You'd better stay at home tomorrow,' she said. 'A rest will sort you out.'

But it didn't. Polly lay silently in bed.

She didn't read, or draw, or listen to her tapes. And, in the end, she started to cry. Round tears rolled down each cheek onto the pillow. 'Oh, Mum,' she sobbed, 'it's all because of *me*..!' Then, in a rush, she told Mrs Peake everything – how, on the night of the concert, she had forgotten her recorder and run back to school for it secretly, while everyone was having tea; and how Mr Mulligan had come limping out in the freezing cold to open the school door for her. 'If he didn't lock up properly it's my fault really, because he only did it for me. And now everybody says he caused the burglary.'

Polly wept for a long time. Mrs Peake hugged her tight and then went away, leaving her to it, because she had something to do.

When, eventually, Polly sat up and

blew her nose, Mrs Peake was back at
her bedside. 'I've phoned the school,'
she said. 'The headmistress says nobody
is blaming Mr Mulligan. Nobody really
knows if the doors were locked or not.
She says burglars can open anything
these days. She wants us to go and see
Mr Mulligan, you and I.'

Mr Mulligan was huddled in an
armchair. 'He can't eat,' murmured Mrs
Mulligan. 'He's so upset.'

'Well, he really shouldn't be,' said
Mrs Peake. 'The police found lots of

footprints on his spotless school floors.
Thanks to Mr Mulligan, they've tracked
the burglars down already! Of course,
the floors are *filthy* now. And nobody
has even put up the Christmas
decorations. Everyone says it won't be
like Christmas at all without Mr
Mulligan.'

Two days later, it was the school
Christmas party. The parents sent along
crisps and cakes and sausage rolls, and

gallons of orange juice. All the children
wore party hats they'd made
themselves. 'I'm afraid Mr Mulligan
can't be here this year,' said Mrs
Roberts, half way through. 'That's very
sad, I know. But something else has
happened that will cheer you up. The
stolen things have all been found, good
as new. By next term they'll be back
again – the computer, the video
recorder . . . Amy, what's wrong?'

Amy was bubbling and popping at the seams. 'Look! Look!' she spluttered. Everyone stared through the grey, sleet-spattered windows into the wintry playground. And there, in his long red coat, hood up to keep out the cold, was Santa Claus! 'MR MULLIGAN!'

Mr Mulligan was coming to the party after all. On his back was his sack, full of the tiny decorations Mrs Mulligan made from milk-bottle tops – one hundred and eighty altogether, one for every child in the school. 'Three cheers for Santa!' yelled Vincent, and everyone joined in the hurrays.

Later, when Mr Mulligan had eaten a big mince pie, Mrs Roberts, the head-mistress, clapped her hands. 'Let's thank Mr Mulligan for coming to our party and bringing us presents. Let's thank him, too, for looking after us all year. And let's ask him if he'll stay on with us next year – and lots of years to come.' Mr Mulligan looked slowly round the room. Then he nodded, and everyone cheered again. 'And, finally,' said Mrs Roberts, leaning towards him, 'let's ask Mr Mulligan what we can give him as a little Christmas present from us.'

Mr Mulligan beamed through his hairy white beard and his eyes twinkled under his cotton-wool eyebrows. 'What I'd like most of all,' he said, 'is to hear Polly Peake play "Hark the Herald" on her Great Uncle George's recorder.'

People turned round and nudged Polly. 'Lucky you!' they said.

'*I'll* do it if your finger's still bad,' offered Vincent.

'My finger's better, thanks,' said Polly. 'But I haven't got Great Uncle George's recorder. It's at home.'

Then Santa Mulligan plunged his hand into his sack and pulled out the old recorder.

'*Oh!*' said Polly.

'We phoned your mum,' whispered Miss Pringle. 'We asked her to pop it

round to Mr Mulligan's house. We
hoped she might persuade him to come.
She's here – look! – at the back, with
Mrs Mulligan.'

Then Mrs Roberts turned out all the
lights in the hall, leaving just the
Christmas tree glowing and twinkling
over all the children and teachers. In
their midst Polly stood up and played
'Hark the Herald Angels Sing' so
beautifully that Mrs King closed her
eyes and thought of heaven. From the
back of the room, Mrs Peake could see

and hear her perfectly and, at that
moment, she thought her chest would
burst with pride.